DISCOVER YOUR FUTURE!

A Fun Guide for Kids to Imagine and Explore Amazing Careers!

Written and Illustrated by

DIVYA MANI

Book Cover and Illustrations by Divya Mani
Written by Divya Mani

First Edition 2024

Library of Congress Control Number: 2024916822

ISBN : 978-1-964416-04-5 (Paperback)
ISBN : 978-1-964416-03-8 (eBook)

Procreate was used to create digital Illustrations for this book
Adobe Photoshop was used to add text to this book

Printed in United States of America

Your Future, Your World

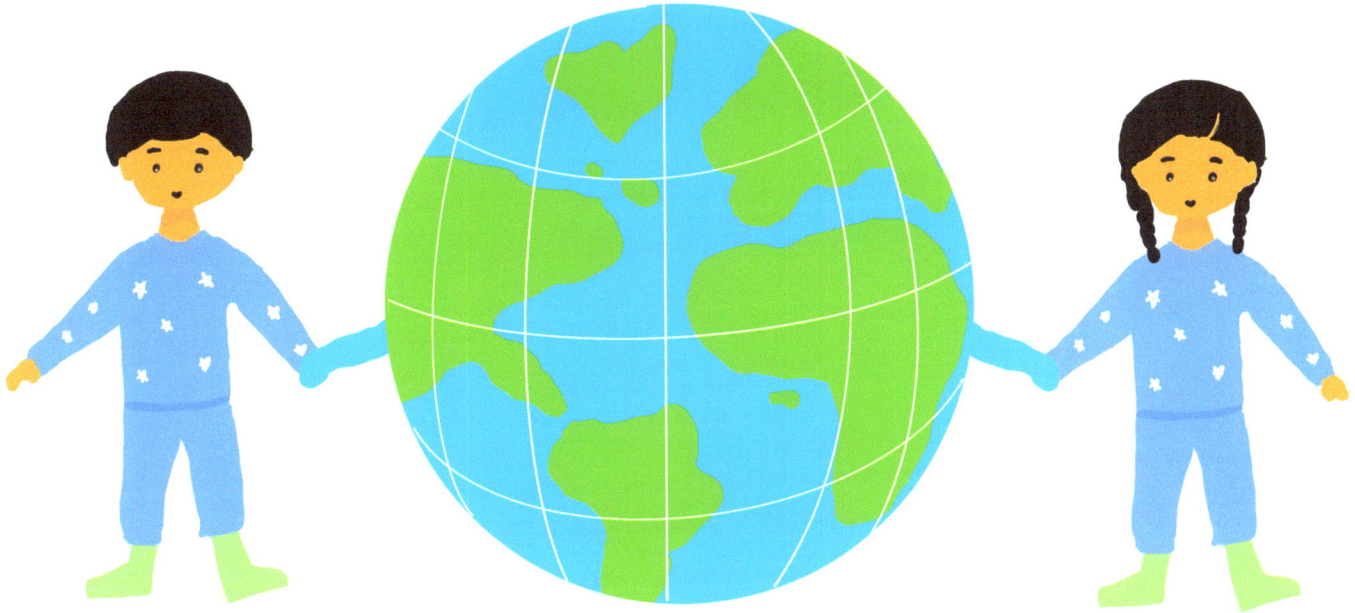

The world is full of amazing things, and one day, you will help make it even better! Every job is like a special tool that can help build a brighter future. Whether you want to explore the stars, help others, or create something new, the choices you make can make the world a happier, healthier place for everyone.

In this book, you'll discover many exciting jobs. But remember, no matter what you choose to be, the most important thing is to always think about how you can help the world and the people around you.

Let's begin our journey to find out how you can make the world shine brighter!

ASTRONAUT

Reach for the stars!

Astronauts explore space and discover new worlds. Who knows, maybe one day you'll walk on the moon or even Mars!

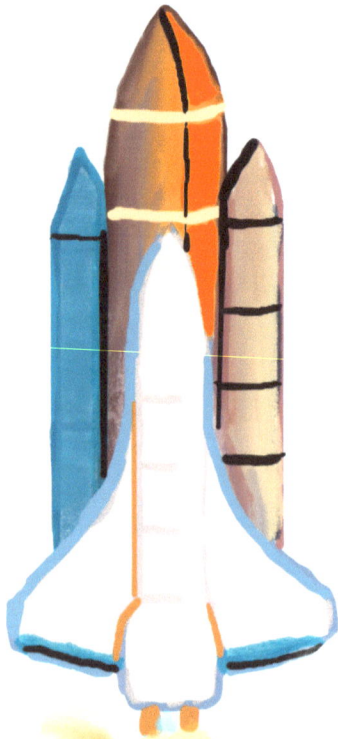

Fun Fact

Space is super quiet because there's no air for sound to travel!

Activity ✔

Tonight, look up at the night sky and see if you can find the brightest star. Imagine flying up there someday—how cool would that be?

If you completed the activity, tick the box ☐

DOCTOR

Doctors are superheroes in white coats! They help people stay healthy and make sure everyone feels their best. Maybe you'll be the one to find the cure for a big disease!

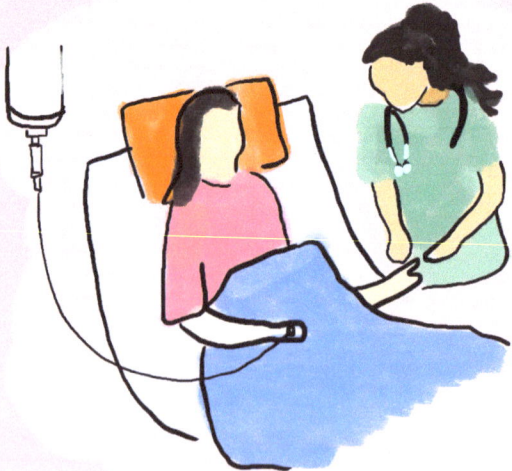

Fun Fact

Your heart works hard every day, even when you're asleep!

Activity ✔

Try this: count how many times your heart beats in one minute. Ask an adult to help you—being a doctor is all about teamwork!

If you completed the activity, tick the box ☐

HOSPITAL

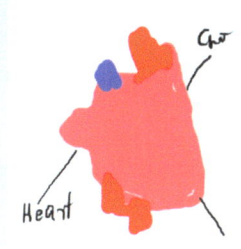
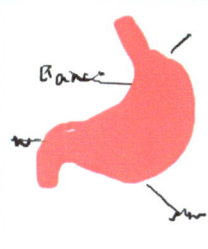
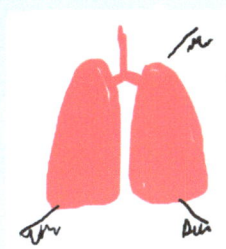

PILOT

Soaring high! Pilots fly planes across the skies, taking people to new places. Maybe you'll navigate the skies and see the world from above!

Fun Fact
The first airplane flight lasted only 12 seconds, but it was a giant leap for flying!

Activity ✔
The next time you're outside, look up. Can you spot an airplane in the sky? Imagine being the one in the cockpit, soaring high above the clouds!

If you completed the activity, tick the box ☐

CHEF

Cooking up magic! Chefs create delicious meals that make people smile. You could be the next great chef, whipping up your own tasty recipes

Fun Fact

The tallest cake ever made was as tall as a house—yum!

Activity ✔

Next time you're in the kitchen, help your parents make a simple snack. How many ingredients did you use? Maybe you'll invent a new recipe!

If you completed the activity, tick the box ▢

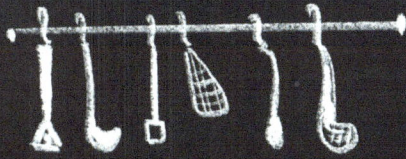

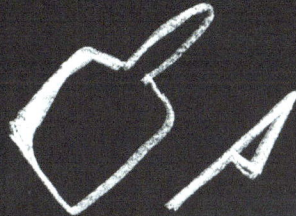

POLICE

Brave and strong! Police officers keep our communities safe. Maybe you'll wear the badge and help protect others one day!

Fun Fact

Police dogs have super sniffing powers—they can find clues with their amazing noses!

Activity ✔

Practice memorizing your home address. Knowing it can help you stay safe—just like a real police officer!

If you completed the activity, tick the box ☐

FARMER

Growing the future! Farmers work with the land to grow the food we eat. Imagine the joy of harvesting your own crops and feeding the world!

Fun Fact 💡

Some farmers grow pumpkins that are bigger than cars!

Activity ✔

Next time you eat fruits or vegetables, check out the seeds. How many different seeds can you find? Each one could grow into something amazing!

If you completed the activity, tick the box ☐

LAWYER

Defender of justice! Lawyers stand up for what's right and help people find their voice. Could you be the one to make the world a fairer place?

Fun Fact

Lawyers learn all the rules to make sure everyone is treated fairly!

Activity

Think of a time when you had to share or be fair. How did it make you feel? Being fair is a big part of making the world a better place!

If you completed the activity, tick the box ☐

TEACHER

Inspiring minds! Teachers help kids learn and grow. Imagine guiding the next generation to be their best selves!

Fun Fact

Some teachers teach outside, online, or even in museums—learning happens everywhere!

Activity ✔

Teach a family member something you learned at school. How does it feel to be the teacher? You're helping others learn, just like your teacher does!

If you completed the activity, tick the box ☐

MILITARY PERSONNEL

Courage in action! Military men and women serve their country with honor and bravery. You could be a hero, defending your nation!

Fun Fact

Some military uniforms help soldiers blend in with trees and bushes, like a real-life game of hide and seek!

Activity ✔

Try standing at attention like a soldier. Can you stay still and quiet for 10 seconds? It's all about focus and strength!

If you completed the activity, tick the box ☐

ARTIST

PAINTINGS FOR SALE

Express yourself in every color, sound, and movement! Artists paint, sing, dance, and capture moments with their cameras. Whether you're creating a beautiful painting, singing your heart out, dancing like no one's watching, or snapping a perfect photo, you're sharing your unique story with the world!

Fun Fact
Some artists use their voices or bodies instead of brushes—just like a singer or dancer!

Activity ✔

Look around your home. Can you find a color, a sound, or a movement that inspires you? Try creating something new, like a song, a dance, or even a cool photo! Share it with someone you love—artists inspire others with their creativity!

If you completed the activity, tick the box ☐

SCIENTIST

Curious minds change the world! Scientists ask big questions and find amazing answers. You might discover something that changes the way we live!

Fun Fact 💡

Some scientists study dinosaur bones to learn about the past—imagine finding a real dino bone!

Activity ✔

Ask a family member a question you've always wondered about. Learning new things is what being a scientist is all about!

If you completed the activity, tick the box ☐

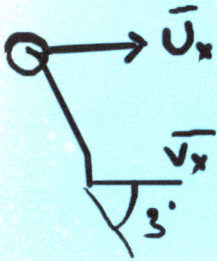

ENGINEER

Building dreams! Engineers design everything from bridges to robots. Imagine creating something that makes life easier for everyone!

$$F = m \times a \text{ (Newtons Law)}$$

$$F = u \cdot \frac{dm}{dt}$$

MECHANICAL ENGINEER

Fun Fact

Engineers help build tall buildings and even roller coasters—talk about fun!

CIVIL ENGINEER

ELECTRICAL ENGINEER

Activity ✔

Fold a Paper Boat! Fold a piece of paper into a simple boat shape and float it in a bowl of water. See if it floats and how it moves! It's a fun way to think like an engineer who designs things to work well.

If you completed the activity, tick the box ☐

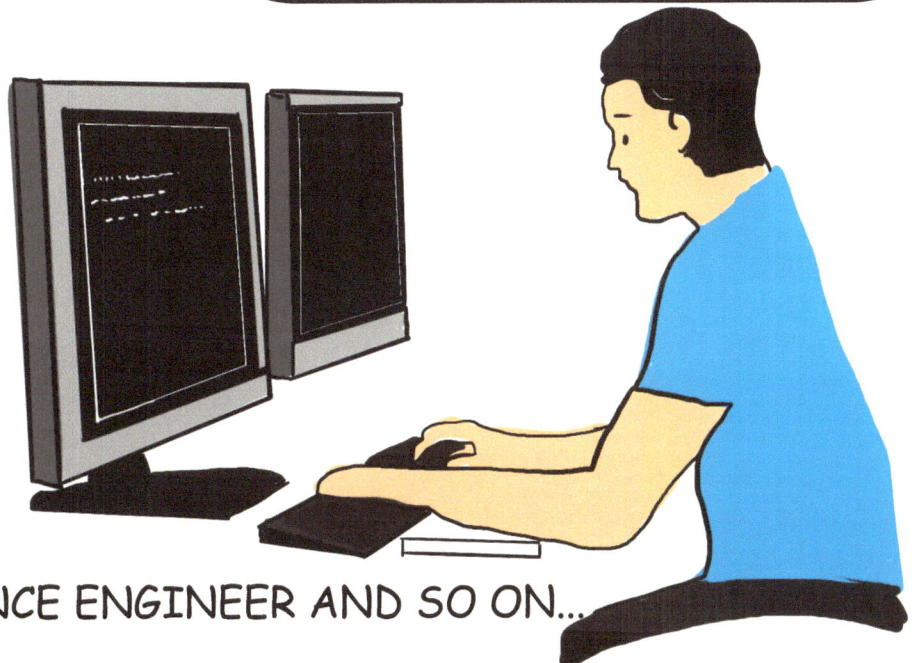

COMPUTER SCIENCE ENGINEER AND SO ON...

BUSINESS LEADER

Leading the way! Business leaders create big ideas and help companies grow. Could you be the one to start the next big thing?

Fun Fact

Some of the biggest companies started in tiny garages—big dreams can begin anywhere!

Activity ✔

Think of something you would like to sell. Share your idea with a family member. What name would you give your business? You could be the next big success story!

If you completed the activity, tick the box ☐

Your Journey Begins!

You've explored so many amazing jobs, each one filled with the power to make the world a better place. But the adventure doesn't stop here! The world is big and full of opportunities waiting just for you. There are countless other careers out there—like becoming a beautician, a firefighter, a veterinarian, an architect, or even an inventor—the possibilities are endless!

Remember, no matter what you choose to be, your kindness, creativity, and courage are what truly makes a difference. Your journey is just beginning, and every step you take brings you closer to making your dreams come true and spreading goodness wherever you go.

"So, dream big, stay curious, and always believe in the power of what you can achieve. The world is ready for you—now it's your turn to shine!"

"What will you be? The future is yours to explore!"

_____

_____

Note from the Author

Hello, young readers! I'm Divya Mani, and I'm thrilled to share my passion for exploring and dreaming with you. From a young age, I gazed at the stars and dreamed of studying space and rockets. I studied Aerospace and Mechanical Engineering and had opportunities to invent many cool things. I enjoyed being an engineer for 15 years. Now, as an artist and passionate explorer, I dive into both the depths of the ocean and travel the world, all while writing books that inspire and excite.

I believe that every child has a unique spark of creativity and curiosity. Through my art and stories, I hope to inspire you to imagine all the amazing things you can become and to follow your dreams with courage and excitement.

Whether I'm painting, diving into the sea, or exploring new horizons, I'm driven by the belief that the world is full of endless possibilities. I can't wait for you to discover your own path and shine brightly in everything you do!

A kind request to parents and teachers: If you enjoyed the book, I'd love to hear your thoughts! Your review would be greatly appreciated and would help others discover the book as well. Thank you for your support and for being part of this journey!

Get in touch: www.divyanatur.com